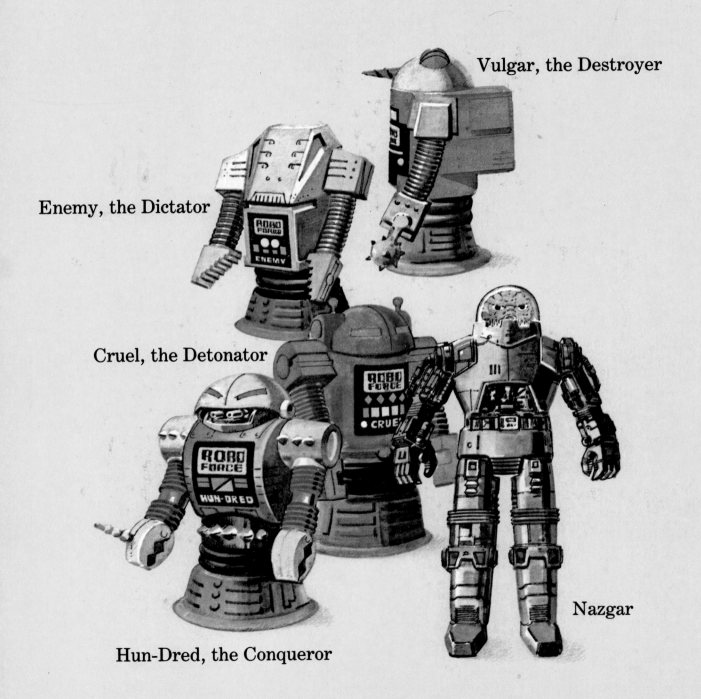

Vulgar, the Destroyer

Enemy, the Dictator

Cruel, the Detonator

Hun-Dred, the Conqueror

Nazgar

Library of Congress Cataloging in Publication Data: Weiss, Ellen. The Maxx Steele trap. SUMMARY: On the planet Zeton, robot servants of the evil Nazgar capture robot super-hero Maxx Steele and attempt to reprogram him to betray his friends. 1. Children's stories, American. [1. Science fiction. 2. Robots—Fiction] I. Mones, ill. II. Title. PZ7.W4472Max 1985 [Fic] 84-18048 ISBN: 0-394-87143-X

Manufactured in the United States of America 1 2 3 4 5 6 7 8 9 0

BLAZER, COMMAND PATROLLER, COPTOR, CRUEL, DRED CRAWLER, ENEMY, FORTRESS OF STEELE, MARK FURY, HUN-DRED, NAZGAR, ROBOCRUISER, ROBO FORCE, SENTINEL, S.O.T.A., MAXX STEELE, VULGAR, and WRECKER are trademarks of CBS Inc. and used under license.

The Maxx Steele Trap
A ROBO FORCE ADVENTURE

By Ellen Weiss

Illustrated by Mones

Random House 🏠 New York

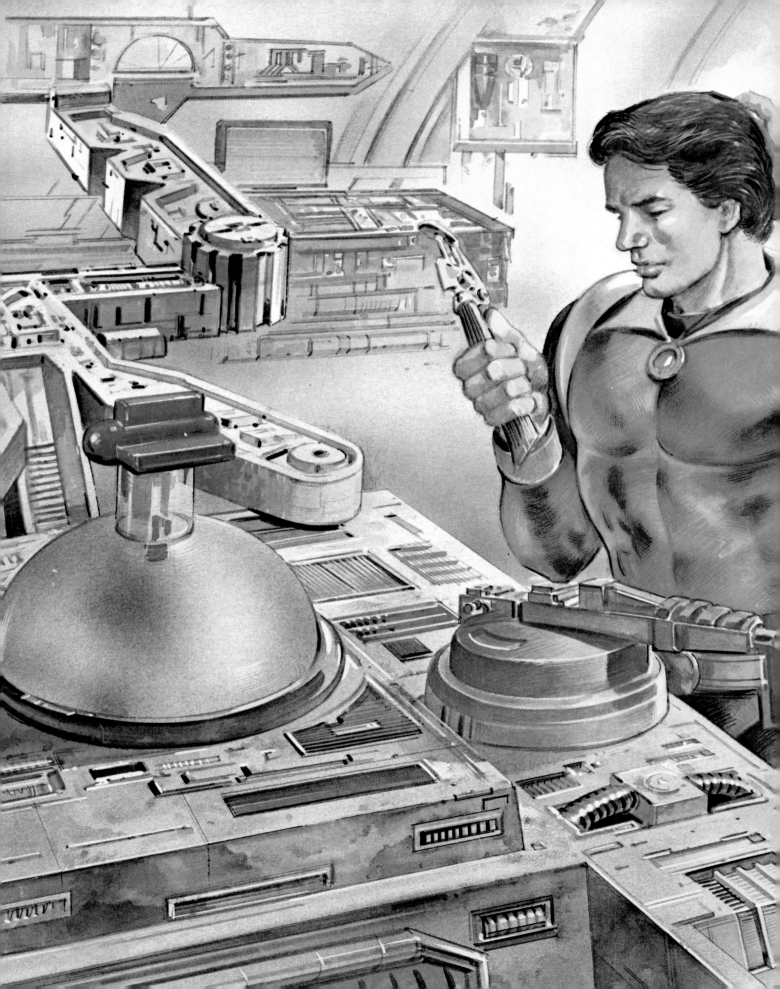

It was evening on the planet Zeton. The twin moons rose in the darkening sky, and the night creatures made strange sounds.

Inside the awesome Fortress of Steele, all was quiet. It was here that Mark Fury and his Robo Force had their stronghold, safe from the evil Nazgar and his henchmen.

Suddenly the silence was broken by the sound of a tool being thrown down a hallway. It took a full minute for the clatter of metal on stone to die down.

"Darn it!" echoed the voice of a very frustrated Mark Fury. "Dumb laser welder—none of these fancy new tools are worth a red cent! Give me a simple, old-fashioned sonic welder any day." He paced his vast underground workshop grumpily. For two solid days he had been trying to make a simple repair on the power system of one of the Robocruisers. But it hadn't turned out to be so simple.

Maxx Steele, always calm, always in control, rolled into the workshop. "You don't look so good," he told Mark. "I think you could use a break. Why don't you get out for a while? You could go for a spin in the Command Patroller."

"That's not a bad idea," replied Mark. "Maybe I really should stop working on the Robocruiser. I'm about to take it apart with my bare hands, I'm so mad at it."

"It's not its fault, of course," Maxx reminded him.

"Well, I'm just one of those crazy humans," said Mark. "I can't be as rational as you." He gave the Robocruiser a little kick on his way out.

"By the way, Maxx," he called back, "would you do me a favor while I'm gone? Check the main security beam outside. I think it might be on the blink."

"Sure thing," said Maxx. "If something is wrong with it, I should have it fixed by the time you get back. We certainly can't have our main defense system in less than perfect shape."

"Okay," said Mark. "I'm going out to do a little hot-dogging over the Poison Desert. Should be back in a couple of hours. Don't do anything I wouldn't do."

"Very funny," said Maxx, following Mark outside.

A few moments later the Command Patroller roared out of its hidden bunker. The air behind it shimmered from the heat of its rear engines. As it took off, Mark began to feel better. He took the patroller into a steep climb.

Three kilometers away, hidden behind a strange sword-shaped tower of rock, was the Dred Crawler.

Inside it was the terrible Hun-Dred the Conqueror. His loathsome sidekick, Enemy, hovered nearby. These were two of Nazgar's most vicious robot warriors.

Hun-Dred took a long look at the Fortress of Steele through his telescopic scanner. He gave a pleased grunt. "Fury is gone at last," he said, gloating, "and the other one is just where we want him. We will have success today—I feel it."

"What you feel is the heat in this miserable corner of the planet. My circuits are already damaged. Why don't you just let me blow the place up?" said Enemy.

"That is not the plan," said Hun-Dred shortly.

"I'm sick of plans," snarled Enemy.

Hun-Dred ignored him. "It's time to go out there and get Maxx Steele," he said. "Let's move."

Outside the Fortress of Steele, Maxx was busy. The main security beam, he had discovered, was indeed on the blink. Nothing major, just a small adjustment.

Hun-Dred knew all about the problem. He had caused it himself, just last night. He also knew that Maxx would have to come outside and fix it today.

Maxx finished the repair job and turned to go back into the fortress. But something bothered him. What was it?

A noise. It was a noise.

Instantly Maxx was on the alert. Every sense was at full power as he scanned the horizon. What was out there? Ah, yes. There it was. The Dred Crawler, undoubtedly accompanied by Nazgar's robot thugs out to make trouble. Well, he was ready for them.

At lightning speed, Maxx calculated that it would be impossible for him to get back inside the fortress before the Dred Crawler reached him. And unless the battle was long and very loud, S.O.T.A., Wrecker, Blazer, Coptor, and Sentinel might not get there in time to help.

But Maxx Steele was a stranger to fear. He stood calmly, waiting for the Dred Crawler, his electron scanner pulsing slowly.

"Interesting," he thought to himself. "Only two of them. Hardly an army big enough to storm the Fortress of Steele. They must want something else." He thought about the problem with the security beam, and in a millisecond he had his answer.

"There is only one logical conclusion," he said to himself. "It's me they want. How flattering."

The Dred Crawler rumbled to a halt in front of Maxx. Looking down from it, laser guns poised, were Hun-Dred and Enemy. There was silence. Even the night creatures had stopped squeaking and croaking.

"Nice evening," said Maxx at last. "Not too cold, not too hot."

"Be quiet," said Enemy, "or I will vaporize you."

Of course, Maxx knew that they hadn't come to vaporize him. If

they had, they would have tried it quite a while ago. No, something else was on their minds.

Hun-Dred spoke in his rasping voice. "Enemy here is rather crude," he said. "Of course I don't want him to vaporize you. And he will not have to, if you'll just be sensible. You know you cannot beat us. All we want is for you to come with us. Just climb onto the crawler, slowly, without trying any tricks, and everything will be fine."

"It's nice of you to invite me," said Maxx pleasantly. "Is there a party?"

"Sort of a party," replied Hun-Dred. "We're going to take you back to our fortress, and then we're going to do things to your circuits. We're going to reprogram you, in fact. When we're done, you'll be just as smart, and just as powerful, but you'll work for us. It won't hurt a bit. You'll see."

Maxx's lightning-quick mind ran down the possibilities. In four tenths of a second he had made these decisions:

1. The odds were very slim that Mark would come back in time to help him.

2. There was about a fifty-fifty chance that Hun-Dred and Enemy together could overpower him.

3. There was something else he could do. He could let them capture him. Inside their headquarters, there would be a lot he could learn—things that would be useful to Mark Fury and the Robo Force. Perhaps he would go along with their silly scheme.

Of course, Maxx wasn't going to let Hun-Dred and Enemy figure out what he was up to. He would have to put up a fight—but not too much of a fight. He wasn't very excited about the idea. "Well, here goes nothing," he thought to himself.

"Work for Nazgar?" he said to Hun-Dred. "You must be joking. I'd sooner be taken apart for scrap metal!" With that, he opened fire on the Dred Crawler with his laser guns. He knew he wasn't in much danger. What they wanted was to overpower him and get him back to their base in one piece. He was glad to help.

There was a fierce battle. Maxx sustained some damage to his left deflector shield, and he did make a few holes in the Dred Crawler. All in all, he was pretty pleased with himself. At last he surrendered.

Just as he was being lifted onto the crawler, the great portals of the Fortress of Steele opened up. Out flew Blazer and Coptor—a moment too late. They fired at the crawler with everything they had, but it pulled away.

"Maxx!" yelled Blazer. "We're coming for you, buddy!"

Hun-Dred looked back at them with an evil grin. "Don't bother coming to get him," he called with a nasty laugh. "He works for us now!"

The sound of Hun-Dred's horrible laughter died away as the Dred Crawler disappeared from view.

Fifteen minutes later Mark Fury returned home. Blazer and Coptor had gathered the others and were waiting impatiently for him.

"Thank the stars you're here!" said Blazer. "Don't even turn off the Command Patroller—let's go!"

"Wait a second, wait a second. Where are we going?"

"We've got to get Maxx back! Hun-Dred and Enemy have grabbed him!"

"Hmmm," mused Mark. "Maxx let himself be captured? I wonder if he wanted to be taken. . . ."

"What do you mean?" asked Coptor.

"Well," said Mark thoughtfully, "suppose Hun-Dred and Enemy came to capture him. I don't know why they'd do that, but just suppose they did. It could be that Maxx saw this as a great chance to get inside their fortress and do some spying."

"Maybe," said Blazer. "But as they were leaving, Hun-Dred yelled, 'He works for us now.' What if they do something to him? What if they convince him to be on their side?"

"It'll snow on the Poison Desert before that happens," said Coptor.

"There's no sense standing here and talking about it," said Mark. "Maxx is in trouble and he's going to need our help. So let's move!"

And with that, Mark Fury and the Robo Force roared off to get Maxx back.

In the smoldering depths of the dead volcano that was Hun-Dred's stronghold, there was frantic activity. Hun-Dred paced back and forth, barking orders.

"Faster, you fools! Strap him into the Cyber Brain! He must be reprogrammed immediately! We must be sure he's on our side before his Robo Force friends get here."

A group of androids wheeled an enormous black machine into the great hall. Three times as tall as Maxx, it was covered with pincers, calipers, and needle-sharp probes. It hummed loudly as it was wheeled in, and the bright blue and green lights on its top section flashed.

Hun-Dred turned to Maxx, who stood watching. "I'm glad you realized it was useless to struggle," he said. "It's all over for you now."

Maxx said nothing.

Actually, Maxx was keeping himself very busy. His eyes moved everywhere, recording data on everything he saw. "Very interest-

ing," he said to himself. "Four or five crawlers, a good-sized computer bank, not many troops. Mark will be pleased."

Hun-Dred saw none of this. He turned back to his androids and gave his final order: "Now strap him in. Tightly. But don't turn the machine on—I want to do that myself."

Maxx Steele looked calmly at the gigantic Cyber Brain. He was not impressed. "Things never change, do they?" he thought. "Can Hun-Dred really be so stupid as to believe this machine can destroy me? He just never learns."

Hun-Dred and Enemy took hold of Maxx and handed him over to the androids. "I've waited a long time for this moment, Maxx Steele," said Hun-Dred wickedly.

Maxx, of course, had to keep playing his game until the end.

"Please don't put me in that thing," he begged, feeling very silly indeed. "Is it information you want? I'll tell you anything you ask."

"Oho!" said Hun-Dred. "So the great Maxx Steele is afraid! Well, I'm sorry, but it's too late. I don't want your information. I want you! You're going to work for Nazgar, Maxx, and you're going to love it."

When Maxx was strapped in, Hun-Dred reached for the switch.

In that last moment Maxx had to admit to himself that he was just the tiniest bit worried. There was a chance—a very small chance, but a chance nonetheless—that he had the machine figured out wrong. If he did, this moment would mean the end of Maxx Steele of the Robo Force, and the birth of another Maxx Steele: Nazgar's most terrible henchman. Maxx Steele of the deadly lasers and double-barreled attack gun. Maxx Steele the indestructible.

Meanwhile, Mark and his Robo Force team were speeding toward the volcano. S.O.T.A., Mark's information-gathering ace, had been picking up some suspicious signals from that direction lately, and it was a prime computation that Maxx had been taken there.

But what would they find when they got there? That was the question that ran through every mind in the Robo Force. Would they find their own Maxx, the Maxx they knew and trusted and relied on? Or would they find a Maxx who had been changed, turned into a robot more powerful and evil than Hun-Dred himself?

An electric storm was gathering overhead. Lightning crackled and black clouds boiled in the sky. The Command Patroller sped on.

"There it is!" Blazer yelled suddenly. The dead volcano loomed ahead, black and threatening. "Let me at it! I'll blast the place to kingdom come!"

Mark smiled a little. "I appreciate the thought, but that wouldn't quite do, Blazer. Maxx is in there, don't forget."

"Uh, yeah, right," said Blazer sheepishly.

"The front portals look heavily armed," said Mark. "We'll have to go in from the back. Wrecker, how about using the old atomic jackhammer to get us in there?"

"You want it, you got it," said Wrecker. "Stand aside, everybody." The noise was deafening as Wrecker's awesome jackhammer went to work.

"DO YOU THINK YOU COULD KEEP IT DOWN A LITTLE?" yelled Mark over the roar.

"Sorry!" Wrecker shouted. "I can't hear you. This thing makes too much noise!"

Mark shrugged and hoped nobody would hear them.

Inside the stronghold, the Cyber Brain was doing its work on Maxx while Hun-Dred watched approvingly. Its hum had been growing louder and louder, until by now it drowned out everything else.

Enemy moved closer to the Cyber Brain, watching it nervously. "Hun-Dred, I think you ought to take a look at this," he said. "It's shaking."

Hun-Dred looked at him with contempt. "You worry too much," he said. "Nothing can go wrong with this machine. I designed it myself."

"But look at it," repeated Enemy. "It's shaking harder and harder!"

Much as Hun-Dred did not want to admit it, the machine really was shaking dangerously.

"Turn it off! Turn it off!" yelled Enemy. "It's going to come apart!"

At last Hun-Dred reached over and shut off the Cyber Brain. Maxx remained motionless.

At that very moment there was a thunderous pounding at the front portals, and then a loud grinding noise as the heavy doors swung open. Hun-Dred wheeled around, to find the arch-villain Nazgar himself standing behind him. Nazgar's brain-dome glowed a bright, angry orange.

Suddenly Hun-Dred was a changed robot. No longer was he the frightening fiend he had been a moment ago. Now he bowed and scraped nervously.

"N-Nazgar!" he stammered. "What a surprise! I mean, what an honor for you to come here."

Nazgar was silent.

"Allow me to show you my new invention," said Hun-Dred. "It will increase your glory a thousandfold." He motioned toward Maxx Steele. "My machine has rearranged his circuits. Now he's yours."

"You idiot! You stupid, silly, dangerous idiot!" Nazgar screamed. "Don't you know what you've done? There isn't a machine on Zeton—in the galaxy—that can touch Maxx Steele's brain! He's a hundred times smarter than you, you fool!"

Hun-Dred was trying hard to look confident in front of his servants, but there was a tremor of fear in his voice. "I have been working on this machine for more than a year," he said. "It is absolutely foolproof. I have thought of every possible way Maxx Steele could get around it. I'll prove it to you. Enemy," he said, "unstrap Maxx, our newest ally."

"Don't do it!" shouted Nazgar. But nobody heard him over the crash of the Robo Force as they exploded through the wall of the great hall, laser guns blazing.

"Maxx!" yelled Mark. "Wake up, Maxx!"

Slowly Maxx began to move. He loosened the straps that bound him. He looked around.

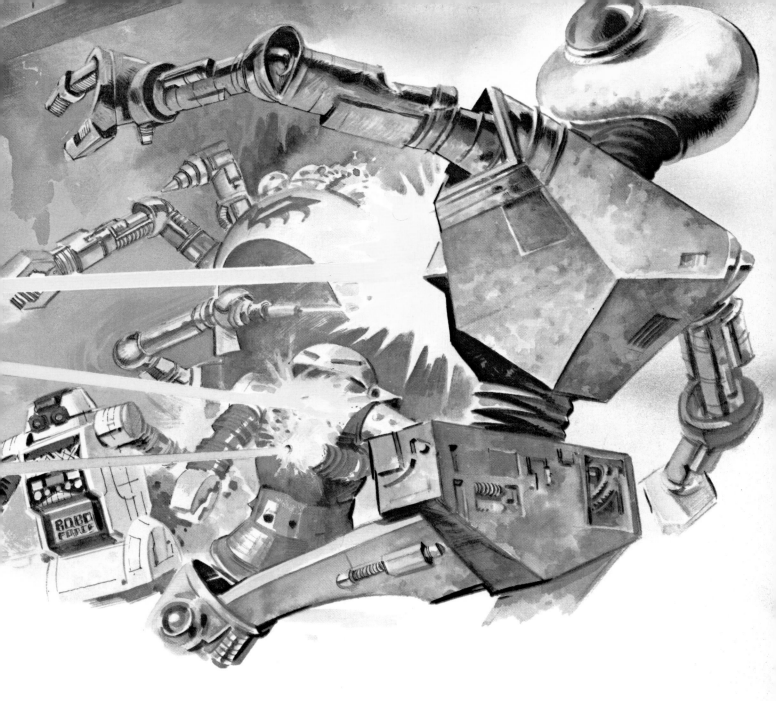

In Hun-Dred's great hall, you could have heard a pin drop. All eyes were on Maxx. What would he do? Which side was he on?

Suddenly Maxx spun around. His laser pistol was pointed at Hun-Dred, and his double-barreled attack gun was leveled straight at Nazgar. "Hi, Mark," he said cheerfully. "Hi, guys. What took you so long?"

Mark could hardly speak. "Are—are you okay?"

"Careful, Mark," warned S.O.T.A., the ever-logical. "This could be a trap. It's possible that he's not on our side anymore."

"I know you mean well, old buddy," Maxx said to S.O.T.A., "but there's just no time to get this all straightened out. Trust me." He did not take his eyes from Hun-Dred and Nazgar for a second. "Blazer, why don't you go over there and take out that computer bank. I'll keep an eye on these two for you."

"Glad to oblige," said Blazer. With one fiery blast he put an end to the computer bank. Hun-Dred and Nazgar could only watch helplessly.

"Now," said Maxx, "let's get out of here!"

That was the signal for bedlam to break loose. Everyone began shooting. Laser fire bounced all over the great hall. There was noise and smoke everywhere.

"Come on, Maxx!" called Mark. "This way out!" Mark made a dive for the hole Wrecker had made, and the Robo Force followed. Maxx came last, covering the rear.

Ducking heavy laser fire, the team sprinted for the waiting Command Patroller. They roared off.

Mark let out a whoop. "We did it!" he hollered. "We went in there and got Maxx!" There was a general cheer from the Robo Force.

For a moment the sound of cheering drowned out the other noise that had begun. That noise was the sound of . . . nothing.

Mark noticed it first. "Wait a second!" he yelled over the din. "Be quiet, everybody." Instantly everyone shut up. "The engines. They've cut out. We've got no power!"

In the moment of panic that followed, Mark found that he was looking at Maxx. So was everyone else. Was he behind this? Was it a trap after all? Had Nazgar managed to scramble Maxx's brains?

The tension was unbearable.

Maxx looked unruffled. "Mark," he said calmly, "weren't you going to get some fuel for the Command Patroller yesterday? I'm sure I heard you mention that we were almost out."

Mark turned red as a desert lizard. "You're right," he said. "I forgot."

"Why don't you flip the reserve switch, Mark?" suggested Maxx, trying not to chuckle. "And, guys," he added, "it really is me. Honest."

"Can you do me a favor, Maxx?" said Mark as he flipped the fuel reserve switch. "Just to set my mind completely at rest? Let me ask you a couple of questions. Then I'll be perfectly sure, and so will everybody else, and we'll be able to stop worrying. Okay?"

"Shoot," said Maxx.

"Okay. What's my father's middle name?"

"Trick question," said Maxx. "He doesn't have one."

"Where's my biggest scar, and how did I get it?"

"You got it when you were six, practicing on your power sled. And do you really want me to tell everybody where it is?"

"I guess not," Mark admitted.

As the Command Patroller roared off into the sunrise, the sound of Mark's voice grew fainter and fainter. "What's the one vegetable I won't eat? What did I hide under the south wall of the Fortress of Steele? Am I ticklish?"

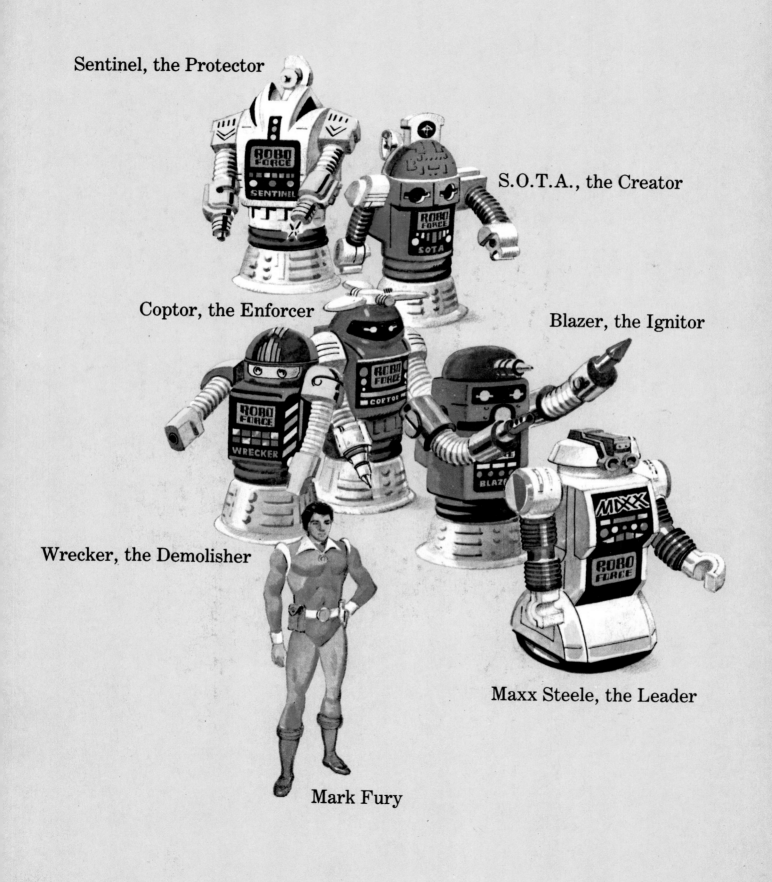

Sentinel, the Protector

S.O.T.A., the Creator

Coptor, the Enforcer

Blazer, the Ignitor

Wrecker, the Demolisher

Maxx Steele, the Leader

Mark Fury